Dear Baby,
It's a Colorful World

By Carol Casey
Illustrated by Jason Oransky

I'm ready to go,
my eyes open wide.

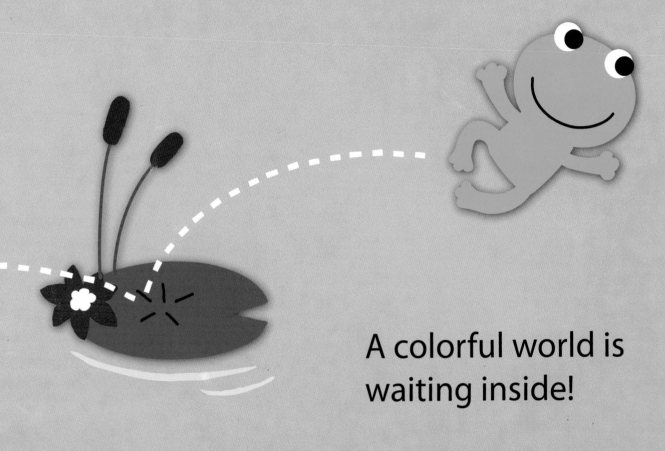

A colorful world is
waiting inside!

Clang! Clang! Beep! Beep!
Sirens passing by.

Blazing, bright, and bold,
Red is never shy!

Little flowers open,
their faces to the sun.

Yellow bees are buzzing
and stopping at each one.

Blue lights up the sky
and shimmers in the sea.

It stretches out forever
as far as I can see.

Pink lemonade on a steamy, dreamy day.

Mama's fancy cake means a party's on the way!

...y bear.

White drifts into the world
for a sparkling winter scene.

Snowflakes in the air feel
icy, pure, and clean.

In wide and dusty canyons,
I see Brown everywhere.

It's comforting and cozy,
like my horse and teddy bear.

White drifts into the world
for a sparkling winter scene.

Snowflakes in the air feel
icy, pure, and clean.

Purple is majestic,
a rich and royal hue.

It's fit for kings and queens
and blooming violets, too!

Bouncing through the world,
cheerful, fun, and happy.

Orange never takes a nap.
It's spicy, sweet, and snappy!

Lying in a meadow
or floating down a stream,

shady trees above me
are cool and fresh and Green!

Let's take a look at the colors of ME!
My skin, my hair,
my eyes that see...

no one's quite like me.
I've got my own look,
my own special page
in life's colorful book.

What if colors were
wiped away?
I think the world would look
sad and gray.

Lucky me and lucky world,
beautiful colors are here to stay!

Acknowledgments:

Jason – thank you for your creativity and hard work. It is a joy to
work together on these books. To my family and friends, your enthusiasm
and support has been a lifesaver. John, you are a great partner and I love you.
And Kara, you came late to the party but your insightful editorial
input has made this a better book. I look forward to our next project.
Sweet Ava, you continue to be my wonderful muse. XXOO

ISBN 978-0-9820972-2-9
Printed in Hong Kong: Publisher Control Number: RPCW0110 First Printing
Distributed by National Book Network 1-800-462-6420
Published by Dear Baby Books www.dearbabybooks.com

For inquiries to the Publisher, please email info@dearbabybooks.com
The author can be emailed at carolcasey@dearbabybooks.com